The Twelve Days of Christmas in New Jersey

by
Margaret
Woollatt

illustrated by
Rich Rossi

STERLING

New York / London

Dear Susan,

Merry Christmas, cousin! I hope your holiday is off to a super start. Mine sure is. That's because, as usual, Mom, Dad, and I are planning a bunch of cool trips around New Jersey. We're just missing one thing: You! Would you come and join us for Christmas vacation? We'll have amazing adventures. We'll take the great state of New Jersey by storm! New Jersey is my favorite place in the whole world, and I know you'll love it, too. Here in the Garden State, we're close to shiny cities and nifty small towns. There are apples to pick, mountains to climb, beaches to comb . . . you name it, we've got it! I can't wait to show you around.

See you soon!
Andy

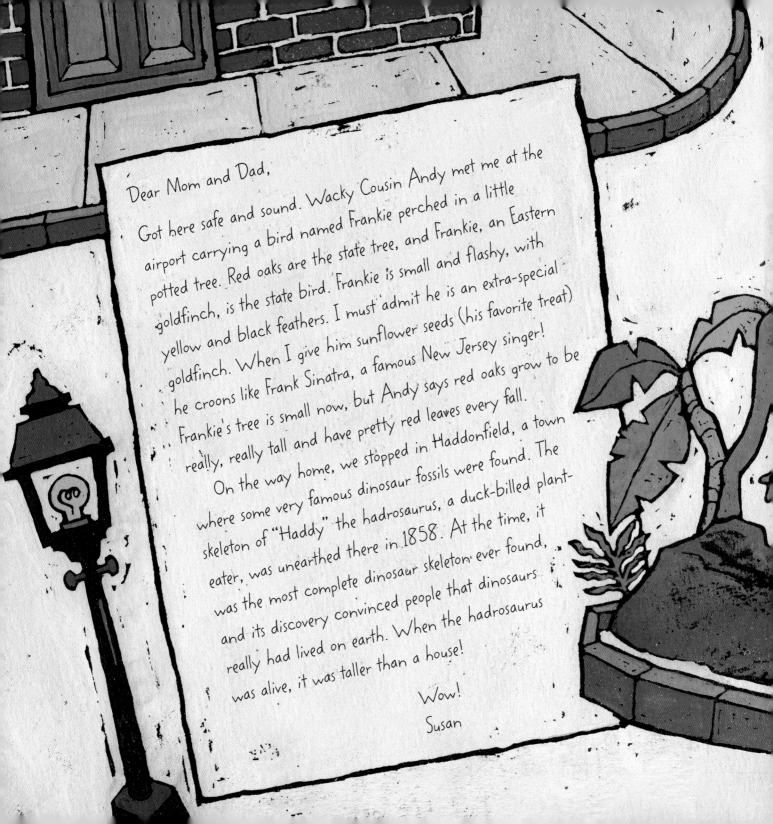

Dear Mom and Dad,

Got here safe and sound. Wacky Cousin Andy met me at the airport carrying a bird named Frankie perched in a little potted tree. Red oaks are the state tree, and Frankie, an Eastern goldfinch, is the state bird. Frankie is small and flashy, with yellow and black feathers. I must admit he is an extra-special goldfinch. When I give him sunflower seeds (his favorite treat) he croons like Frank Sinatra, a famous New Jersey singer! Frankie's tree is small now, but Andy says red oaks grow to be really, really tall and have pretty red leaves every fall.

On the way home, we stopped in Haddonfield, a town where some very famous dinosaur fossils were found. The skeleton of "Haddy" the hadrosaurus, a duck-billed plant-eater, was unearthed there in 1858. At the time, it was the most complete dinosaur skeleton ever found, and its discovery convinced people that dinosaurs really had lived on earth. When the hadrosaurus was alive, it was taller than a house!

Wow!

Susan

On the first day of Christmas,
my cousin gave to me . . .

a goldfinch in a
red oak tree.

My fellow Americans:

Andy and I are patriots tonight! We're all dressed up to look like soldiers in George Washington's army. Soon we'll row across the Delaware River to fight the British. Our password? "Victory or death!"

On Christmas Day in 1776, George Washington led his army from Pennsylvania to New Jersey across the Delaware River. There was a terrible blizzard that night and the river was full of ice. The boats almost didn't make it, but Washington's soldiers surprised the sleeping enemy and won a major American victory in the Revolutionary War. Patriots everywhere cheered! Now, every year at Christmastime, New Jersey celebrates Patriots' Week by reenacting Washington's crossing of the Delaware.

Andy says there were more Revolutionary War battles fought in New Jersey than in any other state. Washington's army camped here lots of times, too. That's why New Jersey is still called "The Crossroads of the Revolution."

Patriotically yours,
Susan

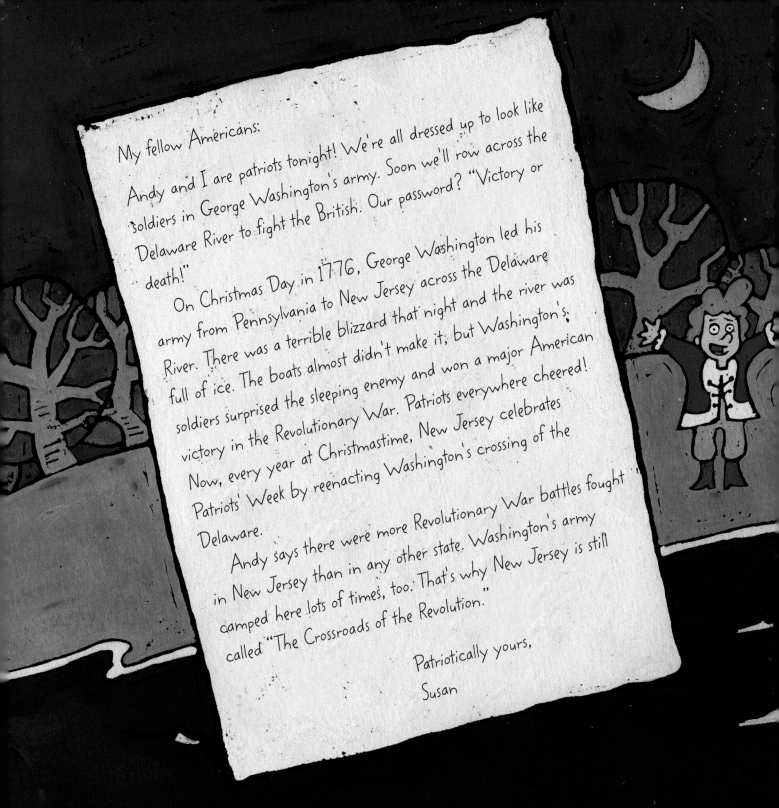

On the second day of Christmas,
my cousin gave to me . . .

2 patriots

and a goldfinch in a red oak tree.

Hi Mom and Dad,

Today three balls of fur named Max, Milly, and Mort joined the family. These are no ordinary pups—they're super dogs! Andy volunteered to raise the puppies for a guide dog school. The Seeing Eye in Morristown trained the first guide dogs in the United States. Now families all over New Jersey raise puppies for this special school. Andy takes his pups to lots of places—even to his own school!—so that they'll be comfortable anywhere. He's teaching the pups to be kind and obedient, which will help them be good guide dogs. In a year and a half, when they're old enough, Max, Milly, and Mort will move back to Morristown. They'll learn how to guide blind people safely on busy streets, in stores, at unfamiliar houses, or anywhere their owners want to go. When they graduate from the Seeing Eye, these super doggies will be lifesavers!

Puppy kisses,
Susan

On the third day of Christmas,
my cousin gave to me . . .

3 smart pups

2 patriots,
and a goldfinch in a red oak tree.

Giddy-up, Mom and Dad!

Andy's favorite way to see New Jersey is to take a ride on the state animal—a horse! The U.S. Equestrian Team trains Olympic horses and riders here, and there's even a picture of a horse on the state seal. In fact, there are more horses per square mile in New Jersey than in any other state. So today Andy and I saddled up some frisky colts and went for a ride. We followed twisty trails through snowy woods, riding up, down, and around beautiful mountains and lakes. We passed lots of pretty horse farms, where horses are raised and raced.

Andy likes getting around New Jersey on a horse, but people here zip everywhere in lots of different ways. Uncle Steve says the state is a transportation hub, which means it has busy seaports, airports, parkways, trains, ferries, buses, boats, bridges, tunnels, bicyclists, tricyclists . . . you name it!

Zoom Zoom!
Susan

On the fourth day of Christmas,
my cousin gave to me . . .

4 prancing
colts

3 smart pups, 2 patriots,
and a goldfinch in a red oak tree.

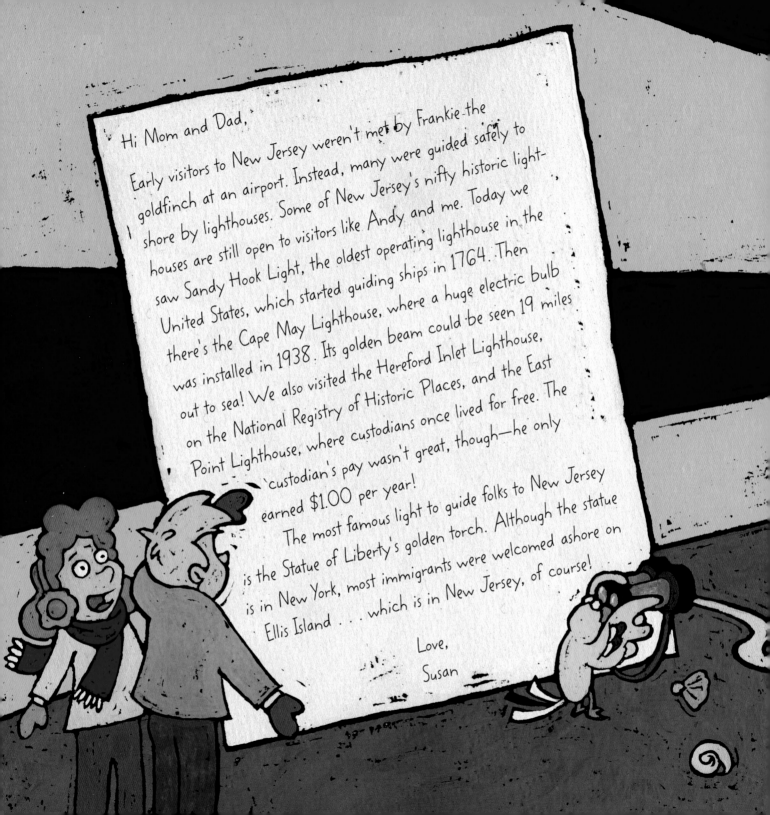

Hi Mom and Dad,

Early visitors to New Jersey weren't met by Frankie the goldfinch at an airport. Instead, many were guided safely to shore by lighthouses. Some of New Jersey's nifty historic light-houses are still open to visitors like Andy and me. Today we saw Sandy Hook Light, the oldest operating lighthouse in the United States, which started guiding ships in 1764. Then there's the Cape May Lighthouse, where a huge electric bulb was installed in 1938. Its golden beam could be seen 19 miles out to sea! We also visited the Hereford Inlet Lighthouse, on the National Registry of Historic Places, and the East Point Lighthouse, where custodians once lived for free. The custodian's pay wasn't great, though—he only earned $1.00 per year!

The most famous light to guide folks to New Jersey is the Statue of Liberty's golden torch. Although the statue is in New York, most immigrants were welcomed ashore on Ellis Island . . . which is in New Jersey, of course!

Love,
Susan

On the fifth day of Christmas, my cousin gave to me . . .

5 golden beams!

4 prancing colts, 3 smart pups, 2 patriots, and a goldfinch in a red oak tree.

Hi Mom and Dad,

Did you know that Andy is an amazing sand castle artist? Beach weather is months away, but he's already built six huge castles to practice for the Belmar Sand Castle Contest. Every summer, thousands of people gather on the beach at Belmar to build the coolest, craziest sand castles you can imagine. Master sand sculptors demonstrate their skills and serve as judges. There are people strolling on the beach, building sand castles. . . . I've made up my mind. I want to be a master sand sculptor!

Loads of tourists go "down the shore" every summer. Visitors swim in the ocean, eat salt-water taffy, and stroll on sunny wooden boardwalks built along the beaches. Atlantic City, full of glittering casinos and fancy stores, also has the first and largest boardwalk ever built. Lots of famous people have spent their summers here. In fact, five U.S. presidents liked it so much they had their own summer White Houses on the shore. Lucky presidents!

Love,
Sandy Susan

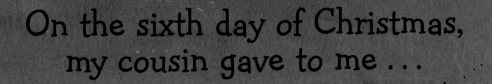

On the sixth day of Christmas,
my cousin gave to me . . .

6 sandy castles

5 golden beams, 4 prancing colts, 3 smart pups, 2 patriots,
and a goldfinch in a red oak tree.

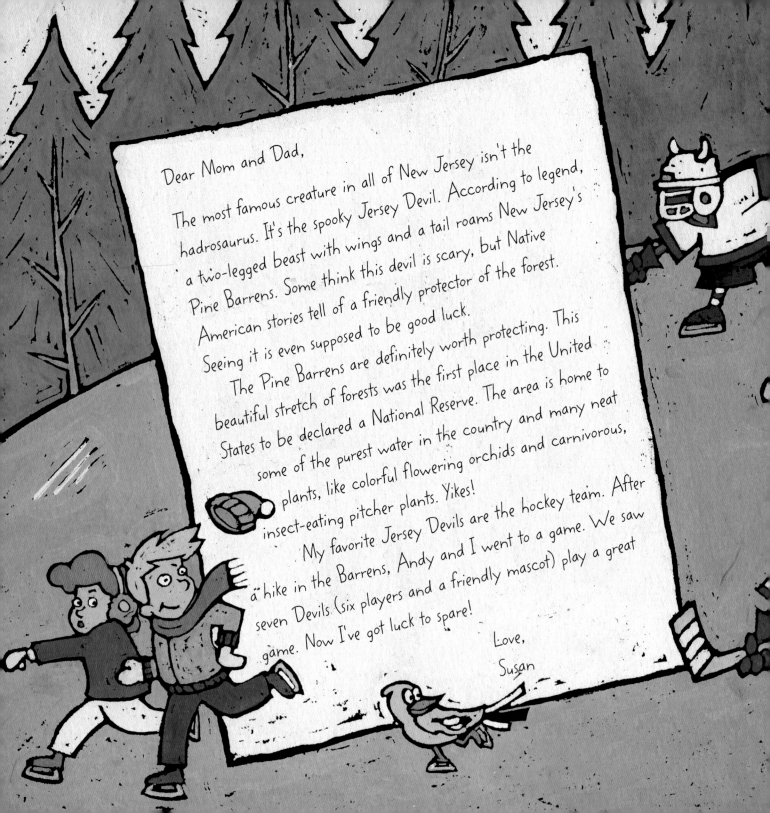

Dear Mom and Dad,

The most famous creature in all of New Jersey isn't the hadrosaurus. It's the spooky Jersey Devil. According to legend, a two-legged beast with wings and a tail roams New Jersey's Pine Barrens. Some think this devil is scary, but Native American stories tell of a friendly protector of the forest. Seeing it is even supposed to be good luck.

The Pine Barrens are definitely worth protecting. This beautiful stretch of forests was the first place in the United States to be declared a National Reserve. The area is home to some of the purest water in the country and many neat plants, like colorful flowering orchids and carnivorous, insect-eating pitcher plants. Yikes!

My favorite Jersey Devils are the hockey team. After a hike in the Barrens, Andy and I went to a game. We saw seven Devils (six players and a friendly mascot) play a great game. Now I've got luck to spare!

Love,
Susan

On the seventh day of Christmas,
my cousin gave to me . . .

7 Jersey Devils

6 sandy castles, 5 golden beams,
4 prancing colts, 3 smart pups, 2 patriots,
and a goldfinch in a red oak tree.

Dear Mom and Dad,

How does a wolf say Merry Christmas? "Arrroooo-woooo!" Andy and I just went to the Lakota Wolf Preserve in Columbia, New Jersey. Packs of tundra wolves, timber wolves, and arctic wolves roam ten acres of forest there. Each wolf has a distinctive voice, so that members of its pack can recognize it. Neato!

Wolves and many other wild animals were pushed out of New Jersey long ago to make way for people. With so many humans around, naturalists are working hard to make sure that animals and wild places are protected. Thanks to these great nature-lovers, almost half of New Jersey is still covered in woods.

Later on we'll visit the Great Swamp National Wildlife Refuge, a spot that several endangered species call home. What a wild day.

Arrroooo-woooo to yoooooooou!

Susan

On the eighth day of Christmas,
my cousin gave to me . . .

8 wolves a-howling

7 Jersey Devils, 6 sandy castles, 5 golden beams,
4 prancing colts, 3 smart pups, 2 patriots,
and a goldfinch in a red oak tree.

Dear Mom and Dad,

Today Uncle Steve took us to visit Thomas Edison's homes in West Orange and Menlo Park. We learned about Edison's incredible inventions. This great genius figured out how to improve lightbulbs so they were safe enough (and would keep burning long enough) for ordinary folks to use in their homes, and he also invented the whole electric power plant system that makes it possible for electricity to flow wherever people want it to go! Edison's first lightbulbs looked a little different from the ones we use today— the glass came to a point on top, like the pointy swirl on an ice cream sundae. Andy and I got to decorate the tree on Edison's front porch with old-fashioned lightbulbs. We were verrrrrry careful.

Andy told me about a whole bunch of other things that were invented right here in New Jersey: the phonograph and motion pictures (Edison again!), the first solid-body electric guitar, the self-adhesive bandage, cranberry sauce, salt-water taffy, and condensed soup, to name a few. What will these New Jerseyans think of next?!

Love,
Susan

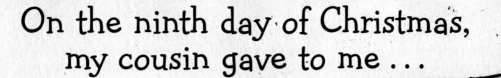

On the ninth day of Christmas, my cousin gave to me . . .

9 lights a-glowing

8 wolves a-howling, 7 Jersey Devils, 6 sandy castles,
5 golden beams, 4 prancing colts, 3 smart pups, 2 patriots,
and a goldfinch in a red oak tree.

Dear Mom and Dad,

Up, up, and away! I have ten new kites and a big head start on the Wildwoods International Kite Festival. Every summer, kite builders, kite flyers, and kite lovers gather on the beach in Wildwood, New Jersey, to put on a spectacular show. Andy says there might be gigantic kites shaped like sharks and dragons, or circular kites that look like UFOs. There could be mini kites on sticks in the sand, floating like a school of tropical fish, or beautiful kites that look like stained-glass windows high up in the sky.

Wildwood has another fun event—the National Marble Tournament. And on Marble Weekend over in Wheaton, artists gather at the Museum of American Glass to show how marbles are made. Visitors get to see experts blow glass into beautiful works of art. We'll walk through <u>this</u> museum very, very slowly.

Love,
Susan

On the tenth day of Christmas, my cousin gave to me . . .

10 kites a-soaring

9 lights a-glowing, 8 wolves a-howling,
7 Jersey Devils, 6 sandy castles, 5 golden beams,
4 prancing colts, 3 smart pups, 2 patriots,
and a goldfinch in a red oak tree.

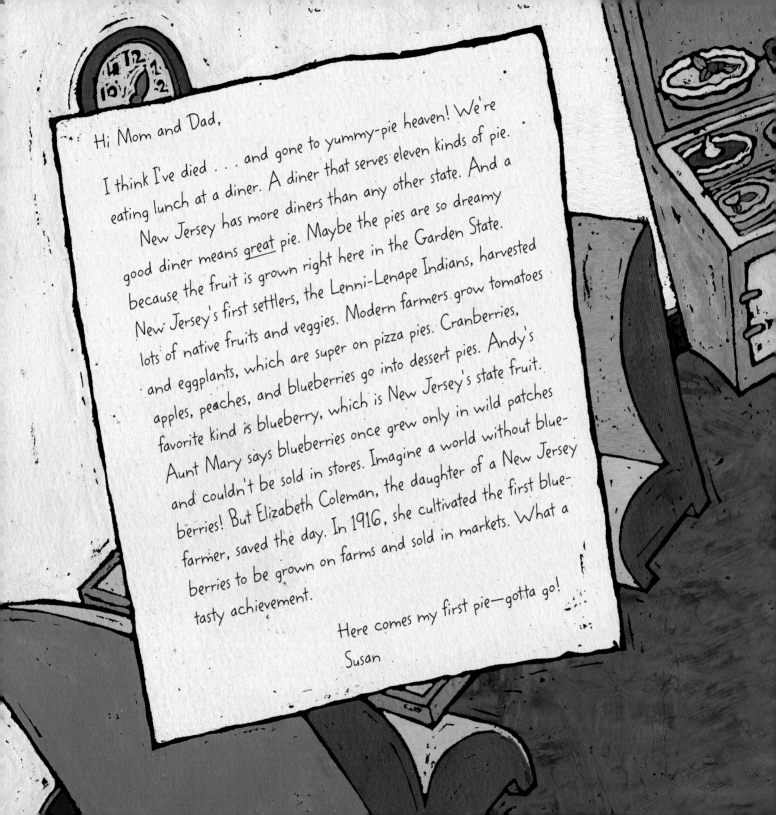

Hi Mom and Dad,

I think I've died . . . . and gone to yummy-pie heaven! We're eating lunch at a diner. A diner that serves eleven kinds of pie. New Jersey has more diners than any other state. And a good diner means <u>great</u> pie. Maybe the pies are so dreamy because the fruit is grown right here in the Garden State. New Jersey's first settlers, the Lenni-Lenape Indians, harvested lots of native fruits and veggies. Modern farmers grow tomatoes and eggplants, which are super on pizza pies. Cranberries, apples, peaches, and blueberries go into dessert pies. Andy's favorite kind is blueberry, which is New Jersey's state fruit. Aunt Mary says blueberries once grew only in wild patches and couldn't be sold in stores. Imagine a world without blue-berries! But Elizabeth Coleman, the daughter of a New Jersey farmer, saved the day. In 1916, she cultivated the first blue-berries to be grown on farms and sold in markets. What a tasty achievement.

Here comes my first pie—gotta go!

Susan

On the eleventh day of Christmas,
my cousin gave to me . . .

11 pies a-steaming

10 kites a-soaring, 9 lights a-glowing, 8 wolves a-howling,
7 Jersey Devils, 6 sandy castles, 5 golden beams,
4 prancing colts, 3 smart pups, 2 patriots,
and a goldfinch in a red oak tree.

Ahoy, mateys!

I can't be writin' a long letter—Captain Andy and I are hunting for pirate treasure! We've found twelve glittering gold pieces so far—and we hope there's more to be found. New Jersey's waters once crawled with pirates like Blackbeard, Captain Morgan, and Captain Kidd. Kidd just might have been the worst of 'em all. He stole treasure from all sorts of ships. Sometimes that mad pirate even stole the ships themselves! British sailors finally caught up with the notorious captain, and in 1701 Kidd was hanged for piracy and murder. Shiver me timbers, what a tale!

But what happened to his treasure? Before he got caught, crafty old Kidd buried much of his treasure on the shores of New Jersey. And it's never been found. Aye mates, not yet.

Captain Susan

On the twelfth day of Christmas,
my cousin gave to me . . .

12 treasures gleaming

11 pies a-steaming, 10 kites a-soaring, 9 lights a-glowing,
8 wolves a-howling, 7 Jersey Devils, 6 sandy castles, 5 golden beams,
4 prancing colts, 3 smart pups, 2 patriots,
and a goldfinch in a red oak tree.

New Jersey: The Garden State

Capital: Trenton · **State abbreviation:** NJ · **Largest city:** Newark
State bird: the Eastern goldfinch · **State flower:** the common meadow violet
State tree: the red oak · **State fruit:** the blueberry · **State dinosaur:** *Hadrosaurus foulkii* · **State animal:** the horse · **State motto:** "Liberty and Prosperity"

Some Famous New Jerseyans:

Edwin E. "Buzz" Aldrin (1930–), born in Montclair, was the lunar module pilot on the *Apollo 11* team in 1969. He was the second astronaut to walk on the surface of the moon.

Clara Barton (1821–1912) was a famous teacher, nurse, and civil rights activist. In 1852 she opened one of the first free public schools in New Jersey. She worked as a nurse during the Civil War and founded the American Red Cross in 1881.

Judy Blume (1938–) spent her childhood in Elizabeth. She is best known as the author of many beloved books for young readers, such as *Superfudge, Blubber,* and *Freckle Juice.*

Grover Cleveland (1837–1908) was born in Caldwell. Cleveland was the 22nd and 24th President of the United States and is the only U.S. President (so far) from New Jersey.

James Fenimore Cooper (1789–1851), born in Burlington, was a popular 19th century novelist. His most famous work is *The Last of the Mohicans.*

Dorothea Lange (1895–1965) was born in Hoboken and became a very famous photographer and photojournalist. During the Great Depression in the 1930s, Dorothea took pictures of people who had no homes and no jobs. Her amazing photographs brought public attention to the troubles of ordinary people.

Paul Robeson (1898–1976), born in Princeton, was the son of a minister who had escaped from slavery on the Underground Railroad. Paul won a scholarship to Rutgers University, where he was not only the top student in his class, but also the first black All-American football player. Robeson went on to become a famous singer, actor, and civil rights activist.

To Meredith, editor extraordinaire
and fellow Garden Stater. — M. W.

To Bobby and Sarah, without whom I
could never be truly "home." — R. R.

Acknowledgments
Many thanks to our superb researchers:
• Melissa France, Youth Services Librarian,
East Brunswick Public Library,
East Brunswick, New Jersey.
• Jo Pure, Librarian, Haddonfield Public Library,
Haddonfield, New Jersey.

Published by Sterling Publishing Co., Inc.
387 Park Avenue South, New York, NY 10016
Text copyright © 2008 by Sterling Publishing Co., Inc.
Illustrations copyright © 2008 by Rich Rossi
The original illustrations for this book were created in India ink
and gouache, then scanned in and altered digitally.
Designed by Scott Piehl
Distributed in Canada by Sterling Publishing
c/o Canadian Manda Group, 165 Dufferin Street
Toronto, Ontario, Canada M6K 3H6
Distributed in the United Kingdom by GMC Distribution Services
Castle Place, 166 High Street, Lewes, East Sussex, England BN7 1XU
Distributed in Australia by Capricorn Link (Australia) Pty. Ltd.
P.O. Box 704, Windsor, NSW 2756, Australia

Printed in China
All rights reserved

Sterling ISBN 978-1-4027-3816-6

For information about custom editions, special sales, premium and
corporate purchases, please contact Sterling Special Sales
Department at 800-805-5489 or specialsales@sterlingpublishing.com.

Seeing Eye® is a registered trademark of The Seeing Eye,
P.O. Box 375, Morristown, New Jersey 07963-0375.
The New Jersey Lighthouse Challenge® is a registered trademark of
the New Jersey Lighthouse Society, P.O. Box 332, Navesink, New Jersey
07752-0332

STERLING and the distinctive Sterling logo are
registered trademarks of Sterling Publishing Co,. Inc

Library of Congress Cataloging-in-Publication Data

Woollatt, Margaret.
The twelve days of Christmas in New Jersey / by Margaret Woollatt ;
illustrated by Rich Rossi.
p. cm.
Summary: On each of the twelve days of her Christmas visit with her
cousin Andy, Susan sends her parents a letter describing the history,
geography, animals, and interesting sites of New Jersey. Uses the
cumulative pattern of the traditional carol to present amusing state
trivia at the end of each letter, and includes facts about the state.
ISBN 978-1-4027-3816-6
[1. New Jersey--Fiction. 2. Letters--Fiction. 3. Cousins--Fiction.
4. Christmas--Fiction.] I. Rossi, Richard, 1960- ill. II. Title.

PZ7.W88175Twe 2008
[E]--dc22
                              2007045845

10 9 8 7 6 5 4 3 2 1

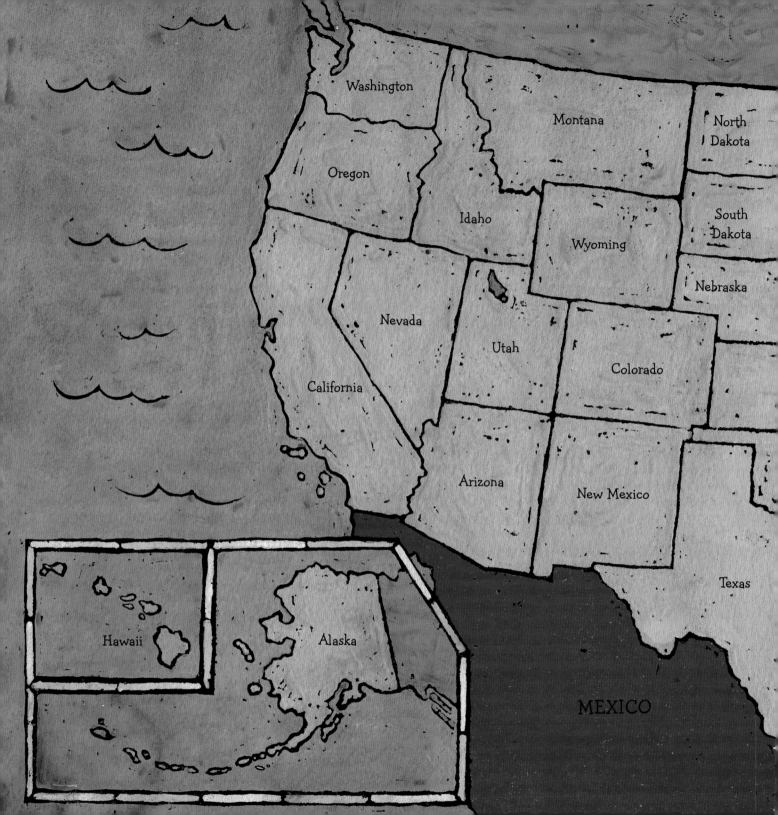